Duck Days

PRAISE FOR *Slug Days*

- **2017 Foreword INDIES: Juvenile Fiction Award finalist**
- **2019 Chocolate Lily Award nominee**
- **2018 USBBY Outstanding International Book**

"A necessary addition to elementary school libraries and a potential spark for a discussion about autism, Asperger's, or simply embracing differences."—*School Library Journal*

"Bender's pencil drawings readily reflect characters' frustrations and other emotions—feelings that Lauren acknowledges she has trouble recognizing. Leach's empathetic novel should both open eyes and encourage greater patience and understanding."—*Publishers Weekly*

"This nondidactic effort is a fine, affecting addition to the literature for kids on the spectrum and for those who know those kids—in short, for just about everyone."—*Kirkus Reviews*

"The first-person narration makes Lauren's logic clear..."
—*The Horn Book Magazine*

"*Slug Days* wisely presents autism as neither disability nor exceptionalism. It's a fact that Lauren lives with; it shapes her encounters without necessarily limiting them. At the book's core lies a wish that anyone can identify with: the need for a friend. This winsome, gentle introduction to differences will be a positive addition to school and home libraries."
—*Foreword Magazine*

"In creating a nuanced, formidable character, Leach tackles a challenging topic with skill and even some lightness."—*Quill & Quire*

PRAISE FOR *Penguin Days*

• **2020 Bank Street Best Book**

"Another fine and enlightening peek into Lauren's unique, often challenging world that displays her differences but highlights the needs she shares with all children: love, acceptance and friendship."
—*Kirkus Reviews*

"While she faces particular challenges, Lauren's misadventures (dealing with loud relatives, letting calves out of their stall, throwing up on her flower girl dress) could have happened to any girl. Other kids will enjoy reading about them from her point of view. Bender's winsome pencil drawings with gray shading illustrate the story with sensitivity and humor."—*Booklist*

"As in the first book, Leach gets into Lauren's head, showing how she feels when others laugh at her for reasons she doesn't understand... Black-and-white pencil and digital illustrations should help early-elementary-age readers understand Lauren's emotions and those of the people around her."—*The Horn Book Magazine*

"Honest and descriptive...In *Penguin Days*, Lauren's family learns to accept one another, no matter how challenging a situation might seem."
—*Foreword Reviews*

"*Penguin Days* provides learning of the most important kind, and has an added bonus of sweet humor, age appropriate text, and engaging illustrations. It belongs on the shelf of every library for young readers."
—*New York Journal of Books*

Duck Days

by SARA LEACH

Illustrations by Rebecca Bender

pajamapress

First published in Canada and the United States in 2020

10 9 8 7 6 5 4 3 2 1

www.pajamapress.ca   info@pajamapress.ca

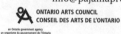

Canada Council   Conseil des arts
for the Arts   du Canada

ONTARIO ARTS COUNCIL
CONSEIL DES ARTS DE L'ONTARIO
an Ontario government agency
un organisme du gouvernement de l'Ontario

Canada

The publisher gratefully acknowledges the support of the Canada Council for the Arts and the Ontario Arts Council for its publishing program. We acknowledge the financial support of the Government of Canada through the Canada Book Fund (CBF) for our publishing activities.

Library and Archives Canada Cataloguing in Publication

Title: Duck days / by Sara Leach ; illustrations by Rebecca Bender.
Names: Leach, Sara, 1971- author. | Bender, Rebecca, 1980- illustrator.
Description: First edition.
Identifiers: Canadiana 20200300156 | ISBN 9781772781489 (hardcover)
Classification: LCC PS8623.E253 D83 2020 | DDC jC813/.6—dc23

Publisher Cataloging-in-Publication Data (U.S.)

Names: Leach, Sara, 1971-, author. | Bender, Rebecca, 1980-, illustrator.
Title: Duck Days / by Sara Leach, illustrations by Rebecca Bender.
Description: Toronto, Ontario Canada : Pajama Press, 2020. | Summary: "Third-grader Lauren, who has Autism Spectrum Disorder, is practicing the skill of "going with the flow," but finds that difficult when she learns that her best friend Irma has made another friend, Jonas. Meanwhile, Lauren is dreading a looming mountain bike day at school. Her schoolmate Dan teases anyone with training wheels like hers. Lauren feels better about Jonas when he tells her how important she is to Irma, and he helps her face the mountain bike day by imagining unkind words flowing off her the way water flows off a duck"— Provided by publisher.
Identifiers: ISBN 978-177278-148-9 (hardback)
Subjects: LCSH: Autistic spectrum disorders -- Juvenile fiction. | Bullying -- Juvenile fiction. | Friendship – Juvenile fiction. | BISAC: JUVENILE FICTION / Disabilities & Special Needs. | JUVENILE FICTION / Social Themes / Bullying. | JUVENILE FICTION / Social Themes / Friendship.
Classification: LCC PZ7.L433Du |DDC [F] – dc23

Original art created with pencil and digital
Cover and book design—Rebecca Bender

Manufactured by Friesens
Printed in Canada

Pajama Press Inc.
181 Carlaw Ave. Suite 251 Toronto, Ontario Canada, M4M 2S1

Distributed in Canada by UTP Distribution
5201 Dufferin Street Toronto, Ontario Canada, M3H 5T8

Distributed in the U.S. by Ingram Publisher Services
1 Ingram Blvd. La Vergne, TN 37086, USA

For my sister, Heather, who is never a big,
messy pain—S.L.

For Weston, my athlete—R.B.

Chapter 1

TODAY WAS A big day. I went to Irma's house
for the first time.

Irma is my best friend. She came to my class
from Sweden last year when we were in second
grade. We both like to search for insects, read,
and make things out of clay. I am helping Irma

with her English, and she is teaching me how to hula-hoop.

Before we left our house, Dad knelt in front of me. "Remember, Irma's family might not have the same rules and routines as we do."

I nodded. "But I'll still use my manners and shake their hands."

"And go with the flow, right?" Dad said.

Going with the flow was something I'd been working on with Dad. It was a new trick he was trying to teach me, to help me not flip my lid, which happened a lot because of my Autism Spectrum Disorder.

Going with the flow didn't have anything to do with rivers. It meant not getting angry when things didn't go the way I thought they would. Sometimes going with the flow was easy, and it felt like I was on a calm pond.

Sometimes it was hard, and it felt like I was on a stormy ocean. But I was so excited to go to Irma's house that I said, "Yes," and started for the door.

Dad held out a hand to stop me. "What will you do if Irma wants to play a different game than you?"

"Irma and I like all the same games," I said.

"What if her mom doesn't cut the crusts off your sandwiches?"

"Irma says we're having Swedish meatballs for lunch. There aren't any crusts."

Dad closed his eyes for a second. "I see you have this all figured out."

"Yes. Can we go?"

Dad stood up and said, "We might as well."

Chapter 2

DAD STOPPED THE car in front of a purple house. Irma sat on the front steps. I leaped out of the car and ran toward her.

She gave me a big hug. "I will show you my insects." She took me by the hand and led me around the corner.

"Lauren, wait!" Dad yelled. "You forgot something."

I looked down at myself. I was wearing all my clothes and my shoes. "What did I forget?"

"To say goodbye." He waved at me.

I waved back. "Goodbye."

"I'll see you in two hours. Remember, go with the flow." He wiggled his hand in the air like waves rippling on water.

I wiggled mine back, then I turned and followed Irma.

She stopped and pointed to the cracked pathway beside her house. "Look at the ants!"

I dropped to my knees and peered at them. Two lines of ants marched in and out of a small crater of sand in the crack. "Where are they going?" I asked.

"I am following them this morning," Irma said. "I'll show you."

"You mean you followed them this morning."

"That is what I said." She took my hand again and led me into her backyard.

She pointed to a candy-bar wrapper lying beside the fence. "My friend left this on the ground yesterday. The ants are eating the chocolate crumbs!"

I looked at the wrapper. The ants marched up to it, picked up a piece of chocolate, and turned around to go back the way they had come. Two of the ants were trying to pick up a chunk that was bigger than either of them.

"But I'm your friend," I said.

"Yes," Irma said.

"But I didn't leave the candy-bar wrapper here."

Irma giggled. "Of course you didn't. My other friend, Jonas, did. He lives in the next house." Irma pointed at the fence.

"But you can't have another friend. I'm your friend."

"You're my best friend. That doesn't mean you are my only friend." Irma took my hand. "I have something else to show you." She led me to the wall of the garage and pointed to the top corner. "Look!"

A bundle of twigs was wedged beside the

downspout. A bird's nest. My eyes looked
at it, but my brain kept thinking, *Irma has
another friend*. I waggled my hand in front of
my face to remind myself to go with the flow.

"Listen!" Irma said.

We stood quietly for a few seconds. Irma's head was tilted so her ear pointed up to the nest. My ears were full of my pounding heart and my brain saying, *Irma has another friend.*

"Baby birds," Irma said. "*Chirp, chirp, chirp.* The mama comes to feed them. But not while we're here. We should go back to the house."

We walked to her back door. It took seven steps. Irma's mom met us at the door. She was a very tall lady with blond hair tied in a ponytail.

She wore a yellow apron with purple flowers on it. "Good morning, Lauren. It's nice to meet you."

I remembered my manners, even though my brain was fuzzy. "It's nice to meet you too, Mrs. Larsson." I shook her hand.

"Would you girls like some lunch?" she asked.

"Meatballs!" Irma said. "Just for you, Lauren."

Irma's mom had stuck to the plan, so I didn't have to go with the flow. The meatballs were delicious. I knew they would be, because Irma shared them with me whenever she brought them to school for lunch.

Irma's kitchen looked kind of like her mom. Everything was yellow and purple, and the table was made of wood that was almost the same color as her hair.

As soon as we finished eating, Irma jumped up and said, "Let's go to my room."

"Dishes," Irma's mom said.

We put our dishes in the dishwasher, and then we ran upstairs. That was something I liked about Irma. She didn't like to sit around at the table after eating either.

Irma's room had a bed and a small table and a bookshelf, just like mine. But she also had a window that poked out over her yard. There was a cozy seat in the space under the window. I climbed onto it and looked outside.

Irma climbed up beside me. "This is the best part of my room. I like to sit here and watch my neighbors." She pointed to the yard on the other side of the fence. "That's Jonas's house."

The yard was empty, which was a good thing, because I didn't want to talk about Jonas the litterbug.

Seven small glass animals were lined up on the windowsill. I picked up the duck. "Ducks have waterproof feathers."

Irma picked up the cheetah. "Cheetahs are the fastest animals on the earth."

"But falcons are the fastest animals in the air."

A boy with lots of curly black hair walked into the yard. He looked older than Irma and me. "That's Jonas," Irma said. "You should come meet him. He likes insects too."

I picked up an elephant. "Elephants cover themselves in mud to stay cool. They live in Africa and Asia, where it is really hot."

"Jonas is an excellent biker," Irma said. "He's in fifth grade at our school."

"Crocodiles have the strongest bite of any animal in the world."

"Let's go downstairs," Irma said.

I wrapped my fingers around the crocodile. "The muscles that hold their mouths shut are very strong, but the muscles that open their mouths are weak. A grown-up could probably hold a crocodile's mouth closed."

Irma took my hand and led me to the door. "He's nice. I promise."

I dropped Irma's hand. I didn't want to meet a new friend. Especially a litterbug. Irma knew I didn't like changing plans. Why was she doing this?

"He won't bite you. He's not a crocodile." She opened the door and stepped into the hallway. Like she was going to go downstairs whether I came or not.

I did some square breathing, which is another trick I use so I don't flip my lid. I really, really didn't want to meet Jonas. But I really did want to make Irma happy, because she was my best friend. Irma knew all about my square breathing, so she stopped and waited while I closed my eyes and breathed in for four seconds. I could hear her breathing with me. I imagined turning a corner and walking four steps while I held my breath for four more seconds. I turned another imaginary corner and I breathed out for four seconds. Then I held my breath for another four seconds as I finished the square. When I opened my eyes, I waved my hand in front of my face.

"What are you doing?" she asked.

"I'm going to go with the flow. It's a new trick Dad taught me. We can meet Jonas now."

Chapter 3

IRMA SMILED, SPUN around, and raced down the stairs. I followed, but I didn't race. I was going with the flow, but that didn't mean I had to like it. She ran outside and through a gate between their two houses. "Jonas!" she called. "Lauren is here!"

I slowly opened the gate and stepped into his yard. A red bike leaned against his fence, and Jonas was putting on a matching helmet. "You must really like red," I said.

"Wanna ride?" Jonas asked Irma.

Irma looked at me.

I shook my head. Irma and I had not planned a bike ride as part of our perfect day. Our plan included looking at insects, making bead bracelets, eating meatballs, and playing with her hula hoop. Definitely no biking. Or playing with boys.

"Biking is fun," Irma said to me. "Jonas puts a...a—what do you call it?"

"Obstacle course," Jonas said.

"An ob-sta-cle course. He puts it on the road. We ride over teeter-totter ramps and go off jumps."

I shook my head again. Irma shrugged. "Perhaps later."

"See ya." Jonas hopped on his bike and zoomed out of the yard.

"Can we make bead bracelets?" I asked Irma.

Irma smiled at me for the first time since she'd seen Jonas. "Yes."

***

My dad picked me up exactly at two p.m. like we'd agreed. Irma and I had finished our bracelets and were practicing with her hula hoop in

the backyard. He waved to us. "Ten-minute warn-ing," he said. "I'm going to talk to Irma's mom." I nodded. That was all part of the plan.

"It's your turn to time me," Irma said. She picked up the hula hoop and held it around her waist.

"Ready, set, go!" I shouted.

Irma swung the hula hoop and started sway-ing her hips.

"One hippopotamus, two hippopotamus, three hippopotamus, four hippopot—." The hoop dropped to the ground. "Good job, Irma! That was almost four! My turn."

I scooped up the hula hoop and held it out around me.

"Ready, set, go!" Irma said.

I swung the hula hoop and jiggled my hips.

"One hippoptam—. Oops," Irma said. "Try again."

I picked up the hula hoop and tried again, but I didn't even make it to 'hip'. I let the hula hoop drop to the ground. "I'll never be able to do it," I said.

"You will," Irma said. "You have to practice. I've been trying for much longer than you."

My dad poked his head out of the back door. "Two minutes," he said.

I picked the hula hoop up one last time and

swung it as hard as I could. It spun around my waist three times.

"That was better!" Irma said.

Dad walked down the back steps. "Time to leave."

I picked up the hula hoop one more time.

"Lauren," Dad said in his warning voice. "We need to go."

I swung the hula hoop. "You need to go with the flow."

He squished his eyebrows together. I let the hula hoop drop and stepped out of it.

"Goodbye, Irma. I'll see you at school on Monday."

Irma hugged me. "Will you come over next weekend?"

I looked at Dad.

"Maybe," he said. "We'll see."

I followed Dad to the car, and Irma followed
me. When I was buckled in, I rolled down the
window. "Thank you for having me."

"Next time you can bring your bike," Irma said.

Dad started the car and we drove off, which
was good, because I didn't want to tell Irma that I
would not be bringing my bike to her house. Ever.

Chapter 4

WE ATE TURKEY burgers for dinner. I liked mine with exactly one slice of pickle and no mustard. My baby sister, Lexi, ate hers in stages. First Mom cut up the patty and Lexi ate little turkey cubes with lots of ketchup. She smeared them around her tray and laughed before she put them in her mouth. Then Mom gave her little pieces of tomato. She threw most of those on the floor.

"When is Lexi going to learn to eat like a person?" I asked.

Mom laughed. "She's learning right now. You were just as messy when you were this age."

"I smeared ketchup on my tray?"

"You especially loved the feel of ketchup," Mom said.

I did like cold things. But I didn't like having dirty hands. "Didn't I want to clean my hands?"

"Yup. As soon as you'd smeared it around the tray, you'd hold both hands up and yell for me to clean them."

Dad swallowed a big bite of turkey burger. "After a while we stopped serving ketchup."

"How was Irma's today?" Mom asked.

"It was fun. She wants me to go back next week."

"That's wonderful," Mom said.

I spread my ketchup into a perfect circle with my knife. "Maybe."

"You didn't want to leave today," Dad said.

"Irma wants me to bring my bike next time."

"That's not a problem," Dad said. "We can put it in the trunk."

I took a bite of my turkey burger. I didn't want

to talk about it. Irma was much braver than me. I still had training wheels on my bike. I couldn't ride over ramps.

I thought Irma and I liked all the same things. But I didn't like Jonas, and I didn't want to bike with him. What if Irma wasn't my best friend for-ever after all?

I swallowed my bite of turkey burger. It hurt going over the lump in my throat.

"Is everything okay?" Mom asked.

I shrugged. "Irma is brave."

"That's good," Mom said.

"But I'm not. I don't want to ride my bike fast or go over jumps."

"There's more than one way to be brave," Dad said.

"What do you mean?" I asked.

Lexi threw a tomato piece on the floor and screeched.

Dad ignored her. "Being brave means doing something even if you're scared. Maybe biking doesn't scare Irma."

"So Irma isn't brave?"

"I didn't say that," Dad said. "I think Irma was very brave when she started school in a new country and couldn't speak the language. But just because she likes to bike doesn't mean she's being brave while she does it."

I chewed my burger and thought about that. When Irma first came to our class, everybody stared at her when she walked to her seat. That would have made me very scared. Just like when I had to be a flower girl at my auntie Joss' wedding. Was that how Irma had felt?

"Was I brave when I was a flower girl?"

"Very," Mom said. "You were scared, but you did it anyway."

"Well, I don't want to be brave on a bike. Being brave isn't fun."

Chapter 5

IN MS. ALLEN'S third-grade class we begin
every day with partner reading, so I start my
school day by sitting next to Irma. There are
some other good things about third grade too.
We don't have to put up our hand and ask to go to
the bathroom. We make a W sign with our fingers

GRADE 3   Lauren

☺
• partner reading with Irma ♥

• "W" sign to use bathroom

☺
• NO Dan!!
☺

☹
• Ms. Allen is loud.

• Ms Allen loves gym
↓ 😫

• gym 5 days a week
😭

and Ms. Allen nods and we leave. And best of all, Dan isn't in my class.

Some of the bad things about third grade are that Ms. Allen has a very loud voice, and she loves gym. She even makes special plans to share the gym with the other third-grade teacher, Mr. Fernandes, just so we can have gym every day. Which means I have something to not look forward to five days a week. She lets me wear headphones to block out the noise in the classroom and I'm allowed to squeeze my eraser, but I still miss my second-grade teacher, Mrs. Patel.

Ms. Lagorio, my special helper teacher (whose name means green lizard in Italian but who is a very pretty lady), knows the same tricks as Dad. When I visited her office in the first week of third grade she said I needed to "go with the flow" in my new class.

"Every teacher is a little different, Lauren. You can't expect everything to be exactly the same."

"But I want everything to be the same."

"Everything? Remember when Irma came to school? That was a big change. But it was good."

"Everything except for Irma," I said.

Ms. Lagorio smiled. "Then you'd be in second grade forever, and you'd never grow up. And Dan would be in your class again this year."

I looked up from the picture of the praying mantis I was drawing. "How did you know about Dan?"

On Friday, Ms. Allen said she had a special announcement. She handed out permission forms.

"Are we going on a field trip?" Ravi asked.

"Sort of," Ms. Allen said. "It's more like the field trip is coming to us. We are very lucky. Instructors from The Real Wheel will be coming to our school and taking our class out mountain biking for a whole day!"

Most of the class started cheering, including Irma. I put on my headphones to block out the noise and to pretend I couldn't hear what was happening.

"You mean we get to spend a whole day mountain biking instead of going to school?" Sachi asked.

"That's right," Ms. Allen said with a big smile. "No reading, no writing, no math. We'll spend the morning learning mountain bike skills on the

field and in the afternoon they'll break us into groups and take us for a trail ride."

"I don't need to learn any skills," Ravi said. "I already know how to mountain bike."

Ms. Allen's eyebrows scooted closer together. "Everybody has something to learn, Ravi. Even me. And I mountain bike all the time."

I lifted a headphone off my ear. Our teacher rode a mountain bike? Teachers were supposed to drink coffee in the staff room and put stickers on worksheets.

Irma put up her hand.

"Yes, Irma?"

"What if you don't know how to bike?"

Why was Irma asking that question? She knew how to bike.

"When we go for our ride you'll be put in groups based on ability," Ms. Allen said.

"I'll be in the top group, then," Ravi said.

"Me too," Alyssa said.

"I am only a beginner," Irma said.

"Do you still use training wheels?" Ravi asked.

"No," Irma said.

I let the headphone fall back onto my ear and squeezed my eraser.

"That's good, 'cause I've never seen anybody trail riding with training wheels," Ravi said.

I threw my headphones on my desk and tore up the permission form. "I won't be in any group," I yelled. "Because I'm not going!" I made the W sign and ran out of the room without waiting to see if Ms. Allen had nodded.

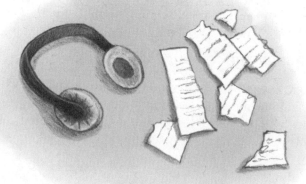

Chapter 6

MOM AND LEXI were waiting for me when the bus arrived at my stop. Lexi was sitting in her green wagon.

"How was your day?" Mom said.

"I don't want to talk about it." I stomped down the sidewalk.

"Lexi learned a new sound today," Mom said. "Lexi, what does a cat say?"

"*Mao, mao*," Lexi said.

I turned around. "Say it again."

Lexi just smiled at me.

"What does a cat say?" I asked.

"*Mao, mao!*" She tried to crawl forward in her wagon.

"You look like a cat, too!" For a whole minute I

forgot about my day.

But when we got home I emptied my backpack and there was a new permission form in my agenda. "How did that get there?" I asked.

"Ms. Allen called. She told me you had a tough after-noon. She put the form in your backpack be-cause she really hopes you'll take part. She thinks it will be good for you to try something new, and to be part of a whole-class activity."

"I'm NOT GOING!" I stomped up the stairs. I wouldn't be taking part in a whole-class activi-ty, because I would be the only one with train-ing wheels. And just like Ravi said, you couldn't mountain bike with training wheels on your bike.

Mom came into my room later, holding her phone. "Irma wants to video chat with you."

I looked up from the paper I was ripping into very small pieces. "Why?"

Mom shrugged and handed me her phone. Irma's face smiled at me.

"Hi, Irma."

"You didn't come back to class today. Where did you go?"

"I flipped my lid," I said. "Ms. Lagorio let me stay in her room all afternoon."

"I missed you," Irma said. "I had to think-pair-share with Alyssa."

"I'm sorry," I said.

"Tomorrow you will come to my house after school."

I looked down at my pile of paper pieces. I knew Irma was asking me a question even though it didn't sound that way. She had learned a lot of English since second grade, but she still had problems with questions sometimes. "Do we have to ride bikes?"

"We don't have to, but I'd like to. I want you to know Jonas. You'll like him."

"I don't think so."

Irma brought her hands into the picture and clasped them together. "Please come over and play! Please! Please! Please!"

A nice hot-chocolate feeling took over my heart. Irma was the best at making me feel better. "Okay."

Irma lifted her hands over her head and cheered. "I will see you at school for partner reading tomorrow."

Chapter 7

AT SCHOOL THE next day everybody was talking about our mountain-bike day. I put on my headphones and pretended I couldn't hear them.

I wasn't allowed to wear my headphones outside for recess, though, because one time I forgot I had them on, and they got caught in the monkey bars and broke. Today at recess all anyone could talk about was mountain biking. And even worse, I discovered that it wasn't just our class who would be biking. All the third graders would be. Which meant that Dan would be there too.

Dan sat with his bum wedged in between two of the playground ladder rungs. A group of kids stood around him, like he was a king and they were his servants. "I ride with my dad every weekend. We ride black diamond trails. They're the hardest."

I stomped over to the sandbox and crouched beside it with my back to Dan. Ravi was there. He had his arms crossed and was making a mad face. "Why are you angry?" I asked. "You're a good mountain biker."

"Dan and I went to bike camp together last summer. He's not that good."

"Are you going to go yell at him?"

"Nope. I don't want to get in trouble from the duty teachers."

"But he thinks he's king of the playground."

Ravi laughed. "You're funny, Lauren."

I stood up, close to Ravi. "What do you mean?"

Ravi took a step away from me. "I mean you're right. He looks like he's sitting on a throne."

"You should be king instead."

Ravi shook his head. "I'd rather make bike parks in the sand. Want to help?"

"No, thank you." I didn't like the feeling of sand on my hands. But I did stay to watch Ravi for the rest of recess.

Mom picked up Irma and me at the end of the day to take us to Irma's house.

Lexi was in her car seat. "*Mao, mao*," she said to Irma.

"Lexi," I said, "this is Irma. She isn't a cat."

"*Baa, baa*," Lexi said.

"She's not a sheep either."

"*Moo, moo*."

"Stop showing off," I said.

Irma laughed. Lexi clapped and gurgled.

"Babies are funny," Irma said.

"Sometimes. And sometimes they are a big, messy pain."

Mom pulled up to the curb in front of Irma's house. I leaped out of the car.

"What did you forget?" Mom called.

I turned around. "Bye, Lexi. Bye, Mom. Thank you for driving us."

Lexi waved and smiled at me. Irma kissed her forehead, which made Lexi gurgle and wave even more. Irma didn't know how much food Lexi smeared on her forehead, or she never would have let her lips touch it. I never did that. I didn't need another ketchup snack.

Mom got out of the car and opened the trunk. My bike was inside.

"Why did you bring that?" I asked.

"Just in case," Mom said.

I tried to go with the flow, but waves started to build on the pond.

Irma pulled on my arm. "Let's check the ant colony."

I ran with her, and the pond calmed down. Mom could take my bike out of the trunk, but I'd pretend it didn't even exist.

The ants had a huge mound of sand in the crack. It looked like a volcano crater. Then Irma's mom came out with a tray of meatballs. She put the plate down in front of us and went to talk to my mom.

"Do you have meatballs every day?" I asked.

"Only when you are here. You should come every day!"

We laughed and laughed and popped meat-balls in our mouths. I wished Dad would make meatballs instead of cheese and crackers for my after-school snack.

As I finished the last meatball, a dragonfly zoomed over Irma's head and hovered above the walkway. It landed on a rock.

"Oh look!" I crept toward it. Its blue body

shimmered like the special metallic paint Mrs.
Patel let us use on our Mother's Day cards last
year. "Its wings look like spider webs."

The dragonfly darted toward the street. We
followed. When we reached the
sidewalk it flitted into the
trees and disappeared.

"Come back, drag-
onfly," Irma called.

"Want to ride
with me?" said a
voice.

I looked up into the tree to see if the dragonfly was talking to us. But instead Jonas rode out from behind the tree.

"Hi Jonas," Irma said. "Remember Lauren?"

"Did you bring your bike this time?" he asked.

I wanted to say no, but that would be lying, so I didn't say anything.

"It's over there." Irma pointed to the front of the house.

Jonas sped to my bike and screeched to a stop. "Nice tassels."

"I can't ride on your ramp. I have training wheels." I turned my back and waited for him to make fun of me.

"I can make a wider ramp if you want," Jonas said.

I turned and stared hard at his face to see what it was trying to tell me. He was smiling, but it looked like Irma's kind of smile, not the smile Dan made when he was laughing at me.

"See," Irma said, taking my hand. "I told you he was nice."

"I can't ride over a ramp even with my training wheels," I said.

Jonas was already pulling a big, wide piece of wood onto the street. "This is perfect."

"I'm not riding a ramp."

Jonas put the board flat on the ground. "This is how my dad taught me. I was scared of ramps, too. Ride over the board on the ground a bunch of times. You can't fall off."

Jonas had been scared of ramps? He looked like he was born brave. Maybe that was why Irma was his friend. What if she didn't want to be my best friend anymore because I wasn't brave? What if she chose Jonas over me?

START

Chapter 8

IRMA HANDED ME my helmet. Jonas
pushed my bike into my hands. I stood holding
my bike, wearing my helmet, and not moving.

Jonas shrugged and turned his bike around.
He rode toward a big jump. He pedaled hard as
he approached it, and his bike wobbled a bit from

side to side. As he went over the jump he gave a little hop and landed on the other side.

Irma followed him. She was able to do the big jump too, only she didn't do any fancy hopping.

I stood over my bike, worrying.

"Come on, Lauren!" Irma called as she biked by me. "You can do it!" She spun around and followed Jonas back over the jump.

I tried to do some square breathing. But pictures of Jonas taking Irma away from me kept getting in the way. I waved my hand in front of my face. Maybe going with the flow would help. Except the pond was turning into an ocean. I wished I had an eraser to squeeze.

Jonas stopped in front of me. "What's wrong?"

I meant to say that I didn't want to ride over

the board. But instead, my mouth blurted out, "Is Irma your best friend?"

Jonas squinted at me. He turned to look at Irma, who was doing another lap. "Irma is one of my friends. But she's not my best friend. That's Jeremiah. Do you know him? He's in fifth grade too. Isn't Irma your best friend? You're all she ever talks about."

Suddenly I didn't need to do any square
breathing or squeeze an eraser. The ocean turned
back into a pond. Jonas' words were like Irma
giving me a hug. I climbed onto my bike and faced
the board.

It was still scary. But my best friend Irma
started cheering me on. So I did it. I rode right
over the board. It wasn't hard. My training wheels
didn't fall off.

"You did it!" Jonas said. "Now do it a bunch
more times."

Irma followed me over the board and we rode
in loops.

Then Jonas said, "Lauren, it's time."

"Time to go home?" I asked.

"No. Time to put something under the board."

My insides went squirmy. Jonas put a small piece of wood under my board and turned it into a teeter-totter.

"I've made you a mouse-sized teeter-totter ramp," Jonas said.

It was smaller than the jump Jonas and Irma had been riding, but it didn't look mouse-sized to me. It looked like it was built for a dog, or a gorilla.

Jonas stood beside it and waved Irma over to stand on the other side. "We're going to spot you so you can't fall over."

I lined my bike up with the gorilla teeter-totter. I thought brave thoughts. I closed my eyes. But that made me wobble on my bike, so I opened them again. I rode toward the ramp. I rode onto the ramp.

I got stuck halfway up the ramp.

"Pedal harder!" Jonas said. He shoved my bike seat.

I pushed on my pedal, and my bike wheeled over the ramp.

"Hooray for Lauren!" Irma yelled.

"You know," Jonas said, "it would be easier without training wheels."

I rode my bike to Irma's yard and sat on her stairs. That was enough being brave for one day.

Chapter 9

LEXI WAS WORKING on her stair climbing. She loved going up the stairs. She loved going down the stairs too, but Mom and Dad didn't let her, because she liked to go head first. We had gates at the top and the bottom of our stairs. But sometimes we opened the bottom gate and let her climb up. Like now.

"Can babies be brave?" I asked Dad.

He stood behind Lexi as she pulled herself up the stairs.

"Good question," Dad said. "Do you remember what I said it takes to be brave?"

"You have to be scared and do it anyway."

"Right. I don't think Lexi is scared of very much," Dad said.

"Why not? She should be scared of everything. It's all new to her."

Dad smiled. "Maybe she hasn't learned enough to be scared of new things yet."

Lexi reached the top of the stairs. Dad scooped her up before she could turn around and belly-slide down the stairs like a penguin.

"I was brave yesterday when I rode over the teeter-totter."

"Yes you were."

"But I'm still not doing our mountain-bike day."

Dad put Lexi down at the bottom of the stairs, and she started right back up again. "If you can ride over a teeter-totter, I'm sure you can at least try the skills course."

"Everybody will make fun of my training wheels."

"How do you know you're the only person with training wheels?"

I crossed my arms over my chest. Nobody else had said they had training wheels.

"Do you want to learn to ride without them? I can teach you today. I know you can do it."

I shook my head.

Dad held his leg behind Lexi to stop her from sliding backward down the stairs. "Okay. Whenever you're ready, so am I."

"I'll never be ready."

"I don't think they make adult-sized training wheels," Dad said.

"I'll be able to drive a car by then."

Chapter 10

THE DAY BEFORE mountain-bike day, Dad
tried again. "Are you sure you don't want to try
riding without training wheels? It will be a lot
easier to ride on the field without them."

I pretended I couldn't hear him while I colored
my beautiful dragonfly picture.

Dad sighed and walked into the kitchen.

Why did everybody care so much about mountain biking?

I went to bed with dragonflies zipping around inside me. When I woke up they were flying even faster.

"Better eat a lot of breakfast," Mom said. "You've got a big day ahead of you."

I swirled my spoon through my Cheerios. The dragonflies were taking up too much space. I couldn't eat anything.

"Your bike and helmet are loaded," Dad said.

I had a plan. They might have signed the form. They might have put my bike into the car. They could make me go to school. But nobody could make me pedal. I would sit on my bike and watch my class. And they couldn't do anything about it.

When we got to school, everyone was so excited about our biking day they were buzzing around like bees doing a dance. Dad pulled my bike out of the car and brought it to the bike racks at the front of the school. I did my best turtle walk behind him. Maybe I could walk so slowly that the bell to go home would ring before I reached the front door.

Irma's car pulled into the parking lot and she jumped out. She ran over and hugged me. Her mom took her bike off a rack on the back of the car and put it next to mine. "Good morning!" Irma said. "I'm glad you're here. I have butterflies in my stomach."

"You do?" I asked. "Why?"

Irma's forehead wrinkled. She made the "worried" face from Ms. Lagorio's cards. "Aren't you nervous?"

"Yes. I have dragonflies in my stomach. But I'm also not going to ride, so I'm not as nervous as I could be."

"What do you mean, you aren't going to ride?" Irma asked.

"I don't want to. They can't make me."

Irma's face turned into the "sad" card. "Oh. I hoped you could ride with me. Now I'll be the only person in the lowest group."

My insides felt like they were being stretched in two different directions. I didn't want Irma to feel sad. But I also didn't want to ride my bike. "I have training wheels," I said. "I'm not brave enough to go mountain biking."

"You were brave at my house. You rode over the teeter-totter."

"But you and Jonas didn't make fun of me."

Irma spun in a circle. "Who's

making fun of you? I'll beat them up." She put up her hands into fists.

I shook my head. "Beating people up is bad. You are not a bad person." I looked across the playground. "But you could stomp on Dan's foot."

Irma giggled.

The duty teacher walked by. "Good morning, girls."

We pretended we were looking for bugs.

"Looking forward to biking today?"

"Yes," Irma said.

"No," I said.

"Oh dear," the duty teacher said.

The bell rang.

"Time to go to class," she said.

My plan to walk slowly hadn't worked. We stood beside the bike racks for a moment.

Dan wheeled his bike in beside Irma's. "Nice bike."

"Thank you," Irma said.

He looked at mine and laughed. "You have training wheels? How are you going to mountain bike with training wheels? You're such a baby!"

My body went hot. I put up my fists. I was going to beat Dan up even if it was a bad thing to do.

Irma stepped in front of me. "Lauren isn't a baby. She's very brave. She went over a teeter-totter at my house."

"With training wheels," Dan said. "That's not brave."

I stepped around Irma. "Brave is doing some-thing even if you're scared. So I am too brave." I moved closer to Dan and put up my fists.

The duty teacher moved toward us. "What's the problem?"

"Lauren's going to hit me!" Dan whined.

"Am not!" I shouted. I put my hands behind my back.

The duty teacher frowned. "Let's go inside. It's going to be an exciting day." She grabbed my hand and Dan's hand and marched us into the school.

Chapter 11

AS WE REACHED my class, Dan whispered, "See you on the field. Baby!"

Before I could do anything, Irma wrapped her arm around my shoulders. "Come sit beside me on the carpet."

My volcano was starting to simmer, but I took

some deep breaths and followed Irma.

Ms. Allen told the class the plan for the day, and then before I could even do any square breathing, it was time to put our helmets on and go outside. I stayed at the back of the line. I walked as slowly as I could down the hallway.

"Come on, Lauren, don't hold us all up," Ms. Allen said.

I swung my arms quickly to make it look like I was walking faster.

On the field we met our three bike instructors. They wore colorful shirts and silver helmets.

One of them described the obstacle course we were going to practice in the morning, while the other instructors rode over it. They made it look easy. There were cones to ride around like a snake, a plank to ride like we were crossing a river, and a teeter-totter, just like the one Jonas had made. Except it wasn't wide enough for training

wheels. I stepped back from the class. The leader kept talking, but my ears were full of a whooshing sound coming from inside me, and I couldn't understand anything he said.

Irma came to stand beside me. "Do you need to do some square breathing?"

I nodded. I closed my eyes and started breathing slowly.

"It's my turn to do the obstacle course," Irma whispered. "You can do this, I know it. Breathe another square."

I did.

It didn't help enough. The whooshing was still filling up my body. I closed my eyes and did some more square breathing.

I heard someone beside me. I tried to ignore them, but they didn't go away. I opened my eyes. Jonas was standing beside me. "What are you doing here?" I asked.

"I'm a helper."

"Oh." I kept counting in and out for four seconds.

"Are you nervous?"

"I'm nervous and mad." I held my breath for four seconds.

"Mad about what?"

I let my breath out. The words tumbled out of me like they were all attached together. "I-can't-do-the-practice-loop-because-I-have-training-wheels-and-everyone-will-make-fun-of-me-and-I'm-not-brave-so-I-can't-take-them-off-and-the-ramp-isn't-wide-enough-for-me-to-ride-with-them-on." I turned my back to him and took in another breath for four seconds.

He didn't say anything for a second. Then he said, "I can teach you how to ride without training wheels."

I shook my head so hard I thought my brains might fall out.

"Then maybe you need to think like a duck," he said.

I spun around to look at him. "You mean I should quack? That's not going to help."

"My teacher says water doesn't stick to ducks. It flows off them. When someone is teasing us, we should let the words flow off us, just like a duck."

"Does it work for you?" I asked.

He shrugged. "Sometimes. It helps when I have friends around."

"Let me think about it," I said.

I turned my bike around so I was facing the parking lot. I did some square breathing. Irma and Jonas wouldn't make fun of me. Did it matter if Dan did?

I looked at the two third-grade classes. Dan was riding around the loop. He ran over one of the cones and he slipped off the teeter-totter. Then it was Ravi's turn. He was so good that he rode over the plank with no hands. And then he did a wheelie!

"Show-off," Dan said.

I waited for Ravi to yell at Dan, but he just rode over to the rest of the class and waited for another turn.

Irma rode around the loop with a big smile on her face, even though she missed two cones and needed help from an instructor on the plank. When she got to the end she waved and pedaled over to me. "Lauren, it's fun. You should try it."

"Dan will say mean things."

Jonas walked over to us. He quacked and flapped his arms.

I laughed. But I kept my feet on the ground.

"Why are you quacking?" Irma asked.

"He's telling me to act like a duck and let the

mean words slide off my back."

Irma waved her hand in front of her face. "Is that like going with the flow?"

I thought for a second. My friend Irma is so

smart. "Yes, it is!"

Irma quacked. "Follow me. We'll go for a paddle in the pond." She rode back to the class.

I stood gripping the handlebars. Could I go with the flow? Could I be a duck? Could I be brave enough?

Chapter 12

I WAGGLED MY hand in front of my face.
I imagined Dan's words sliding off my back. I
looked at my new friend Jonas, who was smiling
at me. I thought about Ravi, who had ignored
Dan. I looked at my best friend Irma, who was
waving me toward her. I stepped on my pedal and

pushed forward.

I rode my bike around the cones. My training wheels got stuck on a cone and tipped it over. I heard Dan snicker. My volcano started bubbling, but I imagined his words running off me like water off a duck.

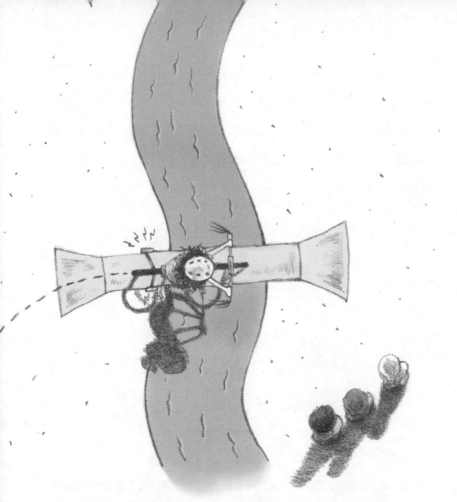

Next was the river. As I rode across, my training wheels ground along the edges of the plank.
Alyssa laughed. But I didn't stop. Her giggles ran
off my back, too.

I lined up for the teeter-totter. It wasn't built for a mouse, like Jonas'. Or even a dog or a gorilla. It was built for a giraffe. Or a blue whale, if a whale had legs. And it was skinny. Too skinny for my training wheels.

Dan laughed. "You'll never be able to get over that."

The words stuck to me. They didn't slide off my back, even when Ms. Allen told Dan to move away from the bike course. He was right. I couldn't make it up the ramp. I wasn't a duck paddling around a pond. I was just a girl with training wheels struggling on a stormy ocean.

Jonas and Irma rode toward me.

"You can do it," Irma said.

"It's just like at my house," Jonas said.

I shook my head. "No it isn't. My training wheels will hang off the side. I'm going to fall."

Jonas eyed the teeter-totter, with his mouth twisted over to one side. "You know how to balance your bike so your training wheels don't touch the ground. I've seen you do it."

"You have?" I asked.

He nodded. "Yup. And if your wheels don't touch the ground, they won't get stuck on the ramp. Start far enough away from the ramp so you have time to get balanced."

"Jonas and I will spot you, like at my house," Irma said.

I thought about it. I twisted my lips to the side to see if that would help me think better. I imagined my training wheels perfectly balanced above the ground. Jonas and Irma stood on either side of the blue-whale teeter-totter.

I spun my bike around.

"I knew you'd chicken out," Dan yelled.

I stopped again. I couldn't do it.

Jonas waved his arm at Dan.

"Can you come help us spot Lauren?"

"Me?" Dan asked.

"Yeah," Jonas said. "You look strong. We could use some help."

Dan scrunched up his face and didn't move. I could feel the waves building in the ocean again.

"I'll help," Ravi said, moving toward the ramp.

"No, I'll do it," Dan said, speeding toward Jonas.

Jonas smiled. "You can both help." He turned back to me. "Ready?"

I turned to face the teeter-totter. Irma flapped her wings. Jonas quacked. Ravi smiled. Dan put his hands out, ready to spot me. I rode fast toward the ramp. For a second, I felt like I was floating. Neither training wheel was touching the ground.

I rode up the ramp. I stalled at the top, but Irma and Dan pushed me back to the center, then Jonas pushed me forward, and before I knew it, I was on the other side.

The instructors cheered. Jonas cheered. Irma cheered and hugged me. Ravi gave me a thumbs-up.

I rode over and stopped in front of Dan. I remembered my manners. "Thank you for helping me."

Dan mumbled something.

I leaned over my bike handles. "Pardon?"

"You're welcome."

His face didn't look like Ms. Lagorio's "happy" card, but he wasn't saying mean things to me either. I decided to let his words stick to me.

"Let's do it again!" Irma said. She rode her bike to the back of the line.

I looked down at my training wheels. Did I want to try the loop again?

Yes!

I rode over to Irma. I flapped my wings and quacked. "My dad was right," I said. "There's more than one way to be brave. But sometimes you have to think like a duck."

Author's Note

Lauren, like millions of children around the world, lives with Autism Spectrum Disorder. She experiences the world differently than some people—it is difficult for her to read people's facial expressions, to adapt to change, and to express what she needs. These differences make life challenging for her, but they are also part of what makes her unique and interesting. We need people like Lauren in our world. We also need people like Irma and like Lauren's parents, who all love and appreciate her for who she is.

Much thanks to Gail Winskill and the team at Pajama Press for publishing *Duck Days* despite the many challenges posed by the COVID-19 pandemic. Rebecca Bender, as always, your illustrations bring the book to life. Sarah Harvey, it was wonderful to work with you again! Hugs to my amazing circle of writers: Mary MacDonald, Rebecca Wood Barrett, Sue Oakey, Libby McKeever, Stella Harvey, and Katherine Fawcett. And love to Heather, Doug, Connor, Annie, Lucy, Johanne, Duane, Ben, and Julia.